The Sleepover Club

Have you been invited to all these sleepovers?

The Sleepover Club at Felicity's

QUICK,
THE TOASTER'S ON FIRE!

by Rose Impey

HarperCollins *Children's Books*

The Sleepover Club ® is a
registered trademark of HarperCollins*Publishers* Ltd

First published in Great Britain by Collins in 1997
This edition published in Great Britain by HarperCollins *Children's Books* in 2003
HarperCollins *Children's Books* is a division of HarperCollins*Publishers* Ltd
77-85 Fulham Palace Road, Hammersmith,
London, W6 8JB

The HarperCollins *Children's Books* website address is
www.harpercollinschildrensbooks.co.uk

4

Text copyright © Rose Impey 1997

ISBN 0 00 716938 8

The author asserts the moral right to
be identified as the author of this work.

Printed and bound in England by
Clays Ltd, St Ives plc

You are invited to a sleepover at
Felicity Sidebotham's

Her address is:
11 Clumber Close
Parklands
Cuddington
Leicester

It is on Saturday 16 November. Please
come at 7 o'clock and sleepover until
Sunday, after lunch.

Remember we need to practise for our
Brownie Cook's badge. And, come
prepared for International Gladiators
in the back garden!

From,
Fliss

Sleepover Kit List

1. Sleeping bag
2. Pillow
3. Pyjamas or a nightdress
4. Slippers
5. Toothbrush, toothpaste, soap etc
6. Towel
7. Teddy
8. A creepy story
9. Food for a midnight feast: something home-made, as practice for our Brownie Cook's badge
10. Torch
11. Hairbrush
12. Hair things like a bobble or hairband, if you need them
13. Clean knickers and socks
14. Change of clothes for the next day
15. Sleepover diary

CHAPTER ONE

Come on, let's go up to my bedroom. My mum's got visitors coming round and she's having a bit of a spring clean. She only gets the Hoover out once in a blue moon, but when she does – look out! She's dangerous.

Dad's in the kitchen making pizza. Do you like pizza? I adore it. I could eat it every day. Come to think of it, I do eat it *almost* every day. That's because it's my dad's speciality. Mum says she married him for his pizza. I wouldn't marry any of the boys I know, even if they made the best pizza in the entire universe. But then I'm not getting married. No way. Not ever.

None of us is interested in boys, except Fliss, of course, but that's only because she's so soppy about weddings. And Ryan Scott. Yuk!

Uh-oh. The Hoover's stopped and I can hear my mum shouting.

"Francesca! I hope you're getting on with your homework."

"Nearly finished, Mum."

"Well, you're not going out until it's done."

"I know."

Better keep our voices down. Mum's on the warpath. She's still in a razz over the *Cooking Incident*. That was so cool. Killing, in fact. Well, it wasn't so funny for Kenny; she broke her arm in two places. But even she says it was worth it. Fliss's nosy neighbours weren't very happy, but then we don't really care what *they* think.

Fliss did care at first. She nearly went haywire. She thought she'd be in doom for ever with her mum and Andy. But in the end even they saw the funny side of it.

The bad news is, we all got banned from cooking, ever again! And you know what that means: none of us can win the Brownie Cook's Challenge. Now one of the crummy M&Ms will win it. They're our biggest enemies: Emma Hughes and Emily Berryman. They're in our class at school and they are seriously gruesome, but there you go. As my grandma says, life's very unfair, especially for children.

I wasn't telling porkies, you know: I have *nearly* done my homework, 'A Day in the Life of a Viking'. Bor-ing. Just sit and wait for me while I finish it and then we'll go round to Kenny's. On the way I'll tell you what happened at our last sleepover. All the juicy details.

Come on, we'll walk through the new estate; it's the quickest way to Kenny's.

Kenny's the crazy one. Her real name's Laura McKenzie.

I've told you about Fliss already, Felicity *Sidebotham*. She hates that name.

Lyndz and Rosie may be there as well, then you'll have met all of us: the whole Sleepover Club, the Fearless Five, as my dad calls us.

And I'm Frankie, the most fearless of all. Yeah! Well, sometimes.

OK, so where shall I start? I suppose it all started the day Fliss called Lyndz 'fat'. Oh boy, was she mad!

We were sitting in the dining hall at school eating lunch; at our school they separate the packed lunches from the school dinners in case the dinner people catch something nasty like mad-tuna disease or cheese-and-pickle poisoning. Anyway, it suits me because I'm vegetarian and I'd rather not sit and watch people eating dead animals, thank you very much. Kenny doesn't mind what she eats; she's a real carnivore. She likes minced mad-cow burgers. Ugh!

One day the dreaded M&Ms came and

sat by Kenny when she was eating roast pork. Emily Berryman said, "Ooh, you've got pig's bottom on your plate." Kenny just lifted her plate and put it under Berryman's nose and said, "You'd better smell it, then."

Well, that spelled t-r-o-u-b-l-e. The plate went flying across the room and both of them spent the dinner hour standing outside Mrs Poole's door.

The moral of that story is: don't tangle with Kenny. She can be pretty wild.

But back to the story.

Lyndz opened her lunchbox and inside she had one of those new desserts. You know those Choc-pots? I love that kind of thing but my mum never buys them. She says they're nothing but sugar and I'll thank her when I'm fifty and I've still got all my own teeth. P-lease!

But Fliss looked at it and said, "Do you know how many calories there are in those?"

Yawn, yawn. Fliss is always turning into

an expert on something. At the moment it's *diets*. She so *stoopid*. I talked to my mum about it; she nearly went ballistic.

"Dieting's very bad for children. You'd better not let me hear *you* talking about counting calories. Growing girls need plenty of healthy food…"

"Yeah, yeah," I told her. "I know that. It's Fliss who needs the lecture not me."

I did try to tell Fliss but she wouldn't listen. Well, not at first, anyway. She just went on pinching titchy bits of skin between her fingers and saying, "Oh, I'm getting so fat." Which is ridiculous. She looks like one of those stick insects Mr Short keeps in a tank in his classroom. Her mum's dead slim as well, but it doesn't stop her doing all these potty diets where you only eat nuts and fruit for a week. We told Fliss she didn't need to do *that* diet, she's a fruit and nut case already.

Well, at first Lyndz just ignored her and scoffed into her yummy Choc–pot. But then Fliss said, "You'll get even fatter eating things like that, you know."

Uh-oh. That put the king in the cake.

"What do you mean *even fatter*?" Lyndz nearly spat out the words. "I'm not fat."

Fliss just smiled and looked away as if something absolutely fascinating was going on at the next table.

"I'm *not* fat," Lyndz said again.

"Of course you're not fat," I said, and Rosie agreed with me. But Lyndz put down her spoon and stopped eating.

That was just the start of it. She spent the rest of the day asking everyone, over and over, "Do *you* think I'm fat? Honestly? Do you? Tell me the truth."

It didn't seem to make a scrap of difference that we all *were* telling the truth. Fliss had really got her worried. The M&Ms came round stirring things up, hanging round our table puffing out their cheeks and rolling their eyes, looking like a pair of bull-frogs. Lyndz was nearly in tears.

The point is, Lyndz *isn't* skinny like

Fliss and me. I'm a walking flagpole, all arms and legs and long fingers. By the way, do you like this nail varnish? It's called Silver Frost. Isn't it drastic? But I can't help being thin, it's just the way I am. Kenny's not that thin and Rosie's sort of in-between, just ordinary. Lyndz is just a bit rounder, that's all. She's got these cute little creases in her cheeks when she smiles. She's got them in her knees as well. I call them happy knees because they sort of smile at you.

But fat she is not. Absolutely, definitely, not on your life is she fat.

After that, though, she'd got it into her head that she was and there was nothing we could do to persuade her otherwise.

Every lunchtime for the rest of the week she and Fliss would sit there reading the back of a crisp packet or a pot of yoghurt to see how many calories were in it. I was getting seriously bored with it all. I mean, I'm interested in food but not in diets.

They're so stupid. It was bad enough at lunchtime, but when we were planning our next sleepover and they started talking about what we could and couldn't eat for our midnight feast, I thought, this has gone *too far*!

"No chocolate," said Fliss, "and none of those cheesy snacks, they're loaded. No popcorn..."

I couldn't believe my ears. "Oh, get a life," I said.

"You can't have a midnight feast without chocolate," said Rosie.

"Cucumber's OK," said Fliss. "There aren't any calories in cucumber."

"Oh, big fat hairy deal," said Kenny.

"No, *small thin* hairy deal, actually," I said.

We both cracked up. But by now it had gone past a joke. It was getting serious.

CHAPTER TWO

The thing is, we all love food. It's one of our fave things. Next to sleepovers, that is. We've all been practising for our Cook's badge at Brownies. And we were going to have this cooking contest. It was Brown Owl's idea. Now she's got back with her boyfriend, she's really cheered up again and we're doing some neat things. We've taken ages to do our Help at Home Challenge, so she suggested, to liven it up, we'd have this little competition.

There's eight of us doing it: the five of

us, the crummy M&Ms and Alana Banana Palmer. We know she won't win, for a start. She couldn't cook to save her life. Whenever she pours the squash out, only half of it goes in the cups.

Brown Owl said, "You can make one thing each – anything, you can choose. You can have a bit of help at home, but it has to be your own work."

I knew straight off what I was going to make, but I kept it quiet.

"I'm making butterfly cakes with buttercream filling," said Fliss. "They're my best."

"Oh, listen to Ready Steady Cook," said Kenny. "What are you making, Frankie?"

"I'm not telling," I said.

"Ooh-er! Get her!" said Kenny. "Classified information. You will not make me speak."

I reminded them it was supposed to be a competition.

"All right. If *you're* not telling, I'm not telling, either," said Fliss.

Rosie pointed out she already had.

"Well, I can change my mind."

So then everyone got dead secretive, which wasn't easy because we're all hopeless at keeping secrets from each other.

Anyway, after that, we were cooking mad. Every time I rang Kenny up, she was too busy to talk to me because she was in the kitchen making some *gruesome mess*, according to her sister Molly. And Fliss kept rabbiting on about these wonderful *novel cuisine* recipes she was making with her mum.

"I don't think that's right," I said. "I think it's *nouvelle cuisine*. It's French."

"Well, my mum calls it *novel cuisine*, so it must be."

This is something else you should know about Fliss: she and her mum are always right.

"My mum hardly lets me do any cooking," moaned Rosie. "She says she's got enough work to do without rescuing my disasters. I have to wait until she goes out, then Tiff lets me have a go." Tiff is Rosie's older sister. She's fifteen, almost a grown-up. "It's not fair. She makes me do all the boring bits like washing and drying the pots, looking after Adam, walking the dog, doing the errands –"

"Oh, poor little thing!" said Kenny, winding her up. "I should ring Childline."

But it's true, Rosie does have to do a lot at home, especially for Adam, her brother, who's in a wheelchair and needs a bit of looking after.

"Oh, my mum lets me do anything," said Fliss, bragging again. "I can make anything I want. But my best recipe is ..." And she smiled that *stoopid* smile she wears sometimes. "Oh, gosh, I nearly told you and spoiled the big secret."

She was just trying to get me going. I knew that, so I ignored her.

And I managed to keep my secret all week, which is some kind of record for me. I suppose I can tell you, though. Not that it's a secret any more. I was going to make pizza. The truth is, I couldn't think what else to make. My dad only cooks pizza and pancakes. My mum doesn't really cook much at all. She says she's a liability in the kitchen. And they both work such long hours that they don't have much time for cooking.

We don't eat only pizza and pancakes; we have lots of nice food from the supermarket. My mum says we should have shares in Marks & Spencer.

My dad says he's probably the world's best chef – at warming things up. "I might write a book on it," he says. "It's very skilled, you know."

He puts on mum's apron and gives us a cookery demonstration, from the best way to open the packaging right down to how to serve it on the plates. He's really silly. My mum says, "Cut out the clever stuff, just read the packet and follow the instructions. We're starving here."

That's one of the reasons I love going

to Kenny's house, because her mum does lots of home cooking. You can smell it the minute you go in the house. Ahhhh, Bisto! You know what I mean?

But once Fliss and Lyndz got started on calorie-counting, everyone seemed to lose interest in our cooking contest. It was the same boring conversation every time food was mentioned. Until I had a brainwave.

We were sitting round our table at school while Mrs Weaver was taking the register.

"I've got this great idea," I said.

"Oh, she's so modest," said Kenny.

"No, listen. We could all do some cooking for the sleepover on Friday. It would be a great chance to practise. We could all make something for our midnight feast."

"Good idea, Batman," said Kenny. The others all agreed too.

"Yeah, great," said Fliss. "We'll finally get to see what big secret Frankie's been cooking up." And she gave me one of her sideways looks.

"I know what Frankie's cooking up," said Kenny. "Pizza."

I was fizzing mad. How did she know?

"Oh, yeah," said Fliss. "Of course, the famous Thomas pizza."

I didn't like the way Fliss said that. I knew she was just jealous. I was proud of my dad's pizza and I didn't want her making fun of it.

"I suppose you'll be making something without any *calories* in it," I snapped back.

"It won't be butterfly cakes with buttercream filling, then," said Kenny.

"Oh, no way," I said. "They're *loaded*."

Fliss went bright pink. She hadn't thought of that.

"Well, there's plenty of nice low-calorie things you can make, aren't there, Lyndsey?"

Lyndz's shoulders sagged. She didn't look as if she could think of any.

The others started talking about what they were going to make, but I kept quiet. I was annoyed because Kenny had blown my secret. But it was too late to change my mind. It would have to be pizza. I'd already asked my dad to teach me and we'd had a couple of lessons. In fact, we were having another one on Friday, just before the sleepover.

That was when I decided to talk to my mum about this stupid diet stuff.

CHAPTER THREE

Me and Dad were in the kitchen, cooking. Mum was washing up. We'd made the pizza dough and it was still rising. So we were slicing the cheeses to go on top. We were making four-cheese pizza, which is my fave topping, and I'd asked my dad if I could take some for our midnight feast.

"Pizza at midnight?" he said. "You'll all be sick!"

"They'd better not be," said Mum, "or Nikki'll have something to say about that."

Nikki is Fliss's mum and she is megahouseproud.

"We won't be sick," I told them.

"Well, OK," said Dad. "We'd better make an extra-big one if we're going to feed all those gannets. I've never known girls eat like you lot do."

"Mum," I said, "do you think Lyndz is fat?"

"Fat!" she said. "Oh, Francesca, don't be silly."

"Fliss told Lyndz she was getting fat and now she keeps going on about diets and calories and inch for pinch and things."

"I've told you before about that," said Mum. "Dieting's bad for you. Especially for growing children. I should think Lyndsey's mum would be very cross if she knew about it. I thought you girls had more sense."

"I *have*," I said.

"People are different," said Dad. "We're not all meant to be thin."

"I know that," I told them. "It was Fliss

who started it. It was nothing to do with me."

"Well, it is to do with you, Francesca, because they're your friends. So *you'd* better talk to them and sort it out."

Just like that, as if it was the easiest thing in the world. Sometimes my mum talks to me as if there's nothing I can't do. It's quite scary really.

"OK. Time to stretch the dough," said Dad.

That's the best bit, where you swing the dough round on your fists. It's ace. It's nearly as good as tossing pancakes. Dad's brilliant at it. I'm not, yet; I usually put my fingers through it.

"You just need plenty of practice," Dad said.

"Oh, joy," said Mum. She was up to her elbows in the washing-up at the time. Good job I knew she was joking. Well, I think she was.

Afterwards, when the pizza was in the oven, I thought about what Mum had said. I didn't know what to do. I needed a plan of action. So I rang Kenny. I always ring Kenny if I want to work something out. I always think better through my mouth, if you know what I mean.

"Hi, Kenny."

"Hiya."

"Hello. Who's that?"

"Molly, get off the extension. It's Frankie for me."

"Oh, yuk *her*!" Then the phone slammed down.

"Kenny, are you still there?"

"Yeah. It's just Monster-Sister listening in. She's gone now."

"Listen, I'm worried about Lyndz and all this stupid diet talk. We've got to do something about it."

"Like what?"

"I don't know, but we've got to talk

some sense into her, tell her she doesn't need to diet. It's turning her into a right misery. We could tell her we like her just as she is. And try to get Fliss off the subject too."

"OK. We'll tell them tonight. I agree with you. Dieting's for idiots."

"You could lose a bit of weight," cut in Molly, "off your mouth!"

"You're dead, Molly! Frankie, I'm going. I've got to murder my sister."

"Call me if you need any help."

Sometimes I'd love a sister. But then I think to myself, I could end up with one like Kenny's sister Molly! Oh, boy. I am so lucky to be an only child. She is gruesome. We call her Molly the Monster. I'll tell you about her another time.

But back to the kitchen. After it had cooled, I put five slices of scrummy pizza in a plastic box. Then I packed up my sleepover kit and Dad drove me to Fliss's in the car.

"Have a great time," he said as he

dropped me off.

"Thanks, Dad."

But then he wound down the window and called after me, "Oh, and Frankie, try and get some sleep tonight."

"Yes, Dad."

Honestly! Do your mum and dad always go on about getting a good night's sleep? Mine do. I can't help it if I'm not a great sleeper. My grandma says it's because I've got such an active brain. She's probably right, because my head's always full of stuff that keeps me awake. My dad says, "Active brain, my foot! It's because she's so nosy; she's frightened she'll miss something if she closes her eyes." He's so cheeky to me.

But sleepovers are different anyway. Nobody sleeps at sleepovers! In fact, they ought to be called *stay-awake-all-night-overs*. That's what we try to do. But don't tell your mum and dad that or they won't let you go to one.

"I'll try," I called back. "It's the others,

they keep me awake." And I smiled and waved, as if four-cheese pizza wouldn't melt in my mouth.

CHAPTER FOUR

When I rang the bell, Fliss's mum opened the door.

"Hello, Francesca. Take your shoes off, dear, and then you can go on up. Everyone else is here. Shall I take that box from you?"

"No, thanks, Mrs Sidebotham. It's just got a few bits of pizza in it."

"A few bits of pizza for a midnight feast, I'll bet," she said, smiling. "You'll try not to make a mess, won't you, sweetheart?"

I smiled and nodded. After all, we were going to eat it, not spread it on the carpet.

But as I've already told you, we have to be mega-careful at Fliss's house. I'd probably better tell you a bit about Fliss and her family next, then you'll understand why what happened later was such a D-for-disaster.

Fliss lives with her mum and her brother Callum – he's only seven and a bit of a pest – and Andy, her mum's boyfriend. Her dad lives just round the corner, with his girlfriend and her little boy and their new baby, Posie. She is so *cute*.

If you went to Fliss's house you would think she was dead posh, but she's not. It's just that her mum likes everything sparkly clean and neat and tidy. And cream! That's the other thing: everything's cream. The sofa, the curtains, even the carpet. So you have to take your shoes off the minute you go in. And you have to be on guard against spilling anything, or breaking anything, or scruffing anything up, unless you're in

Fliss's room or out in the garden. Then you can relax.

The lounge has got huge patio doors and the kitchen is like something in a TV ad. It's all shiny and new-looking and – you've guessed it – cream!

It's not a bit like my house. For a start, there are no piles of papers covering the table at Fliss's. No books, no newspapers all over the place. And no dog either.

Fliss would love a pet but the only one she's allowed is a goldfish called Bubbles. That's because goldfish don't leave hairs on the carpets. They don't do any other unmentionable things either! Well, I suppose they do but it just falls to the bottom of the bowl, until you clean it out.

Fliss's mum works at home. She does facials and massage and things. Fliss says she's a beauty technician. She also teaches keep-fit and aerobics. Andy is a plasterer. We don't see much of him because he works all the time.

The best thing about Fliss's house is

the whirlpool bath with its own Jacuzzi. It's ace. Guess what colour it is! No, you're wrong, actually. It's pink with gold taps.

The worst thing about Fliss's house is the people next door. The Grumpies.

That's what we call them. They're really called Charles and Jessica Watson-Wade and Baby Bruno. Honestly, I didn't make that up. Fliss's mum tries to be nice and get along with them but they're so stuck up and they're always complaining.

If Callum plays in the garden with his friends, it gives Mrs Watson-Wade a migraine.

If Fliss plays her tapes in her bedroom, it wakes Baby Bruno up.

If Andy doesn't cut the front hedge, it spoils the view from their lounge window.

They are seriously horrible.

So one of our hobbies, when we go to Fliss's, is winding up the Watson-Wades.

Sometimes we spy on them through a hole in the fence. Mrs Grumpy is mad about sunbathing and in the summer Fliss once saw her with nothing on. Well, that's what *she* said, but you can't believe everything Fliss tells you.

Lately, though, we've been annoying Mr Grumpy by setting off his car alarm. We got away with it the first few times, but last time he knew it was us and gave us this big lecture. He told us we were very naughty girls and we'd probably grow up to be vandals. We'd only set his car alarm off!

The Grumpies have got this *perfect* garden and *perfect* pond with dead-expensive carp in it. Mr Grumpy's always fishing out the leaves and the weeds. He even cuts the grass round it with a pair of scissors. We've seen him. He's always bragging about how it's his pride and joy. So we roll up bus tickets and sweet papers and push them through the hole in the fence, hoping they'll land in the pond on the other side. Then we watch him fishing them out. You can see him frowning, wondering where they've come from. We have to keep really quiet so he won't hear us laughing. Otherwise we'd get another lecture.

But we did something much worse than that this time. Oh, it was brilliant. They're never going to forgive us. No way. We're in serious doom with the Grumpies now.

After Fliss's mum let me in, I went upstairs and found the others all sitting on Fliss's bed. There were sleeping bags all over the room and plastic boxes of food and everybody's sleepover kits. I could only just get in.

"Hi, Frankie," said Kenny. "Show us what you've brought."

"The Authentic Thomas Four-Cheese Pizza," I said, opening the lid.

"Mmmm!" said Kenny. "Smells heavenly." *Heavenly* is Kenny's favourite word.

"Four-cheese!" said Fliss. "Do you realise how many calories that is?"

"Oh, don't start," I warned her.

She just shrugged and looked away.

"I brought flapjack," said Kenny. "My gran's recipe."

"Brown-sugar flapjack. Oh, Kenny, all those calories!" I said, grinning.

"Rosie's brought cheese straws," said Kenny.

"More cheese," Fliss muttered.

"What about you?" I asked Lyndz.

But Fliss spoke for her. "Lyndz has made popcorn and I've made a lemon surprise."

Well, that sounded OK. But all this talk about food was making me hungry. I didn't think I could wait till midnight.

"Why don't we have some now?" I suggested.

"You know the rules," said Fliss.

Fliss is pretty bossy most of the time, and when the sleepover's at her house there's no living with her. She's very strict about rules.

One of our rules is that we save our food until we're all in bed and it's dark.

We hardly ever manage to wait until midnight. But we try not to eat it too early.

"Anyway," she said, "I was just showing Rosie my room."

Uh-oh. Bor-ing. The grand tour of Fliss's bedroom was about to start.

CHAPTER FIVE

Rosie had never been to Fliss's house before because she was new to the Sleepover Club, so Fliss *had* to show her everything: all her ornaments, all her soft toys and the entire contents of her wardrobe. Fliss's got loads of clothes. I could see she was in a real showing-off mood, trying to impress Rosie. Not only has she got a lot of clothes, they're all hanging up or folded neatly, arranged according to colour. Sweaters, T-shirts, leggings, skirts, all colour-coordinated, and her shoes and boots lined up in pairs.

It looks like Sindy's wardrobe.

"Do you want to wear something of mine?" Fliss asked.

"Can I?" said Rosie, her eyes nearly popping out.

"I don't mind," said Fliss. "Anybody can borrow anything they like."

Well, she knows I'm too tall to get into anything of hers and Kenny only wears her Leicester City football shirt anyway. But Rosie borrowed her Ton-Sur-Ton tracksuit. It just fitted her because it was a bit sloppy on Fliss.

Lyndsey had gone all quiet and was looking really miserable again. I knew what that was about. I started thinking about what my mum had said and what she expected me to do about it.

"Do *you* want to borrow anything?" Fliss asked Lyndz.

Lyndsey shook her head.

"You'll soon fit in them, if you keep to the diet," said Fliss smugly.

"I hope you're not seriously on a diet,"

I said. "Diets are bad for you."

"Diets are for idiots," said Kenny.

"It's not really a diet," she said, but she'd gone all pink, so we knew it was a bit of a porky pie.

"Well, it'd better not be," I said. "Your mum would go mad if she knew. Just because Fliss is thin, there's no reason why you should be. It's stupid wanting to look like someone else. We're all different. You should be happy with the way you are. My grandma says, 'Comparison is a useless exercise'."

"Ooo-er! Get her!" said Kenny. "Frankie swallowed a dictionary."

It was quite a little speech and everyone looked at me as if I'd had a brain transplant.

"It's all right for you, Frankie," said Lyndsey. "You're tall and thin."

"Look," I said. "D'you suppose I like being this tall? Sometimes it really gets on my wires. Don't you think I'd like to be the same size as the rest of you? But what's the point of whingeing about it? I'm tall. There's nothing I can do about it."

I was feeling dead hot and embarrassed. I just wanted a hole to open up in the floor and swallow me. But then Kenny started up and made everything OK.

"Yeah," said Kenny, "Frankie's right. We're all different. D'you suppose I like being this gorgeous? Don't you think sometimes I'd like to be dead plain and ugly like the rest of you? It isn't easy being stunningly beautiful, you know. But I am. There's nothing I can do about that."

She was pulling stupid faces and posing, as if she was being photographed for *Just Seventeen*. Sometimes Kenny is so embarrassing she really makes us squeal. This was one of those times. She even made Lyndsey smile.

"You are too crazy to live," I said. And we set on her with our pillows.

"Oh, be careful!" said Fliss. "You might break something."

Well, she was right. Her room's pretty small and there isn't room to swing a cat, never mind a squishy-poo. A squishy-poo, by the way, is a sleeping bag filled with clothes and things so it makes a sort of *humungous* pillow for whacking people with. But before we could make one, Fliss said, "Let's go into the garden."

So we all got up and headed off downstairs for a round of International Gladiators on Fliss's back lawn.

"Don't make too much noise and annoy the neighbours," Fliss's mum called out from the lounge. "You know what they're like."

"Yes, Mum," Fliss called back. And we all grinned. We knew exactly what they were like. The Gruesome Grumples.

Fliss's garden is dead neat and tidy, just like her house. We're allowed on the lawn, but we're not supposed to go on the flowerbeds, which is a bit of a problem when you're having *barging contests*.

This is what we do: first we get into pairs. One of us is the horse and the other's the rider. If you're the rider, you have to hold on tight and concentrate on staying on. If you're the horse, you have to barge into the other horse and try to push it off the grass. You can't use your hands *at all* and kicking is *not* allowed. Whoever's left out has to be the referee and see that nobody breaks the rules and decide who's the winner.

Actually it's not my favourite contest. Because I'm so much bigger than the others, I never get to be a rider. Kenny's a good sport and she did try once or twice to carry me but she just buckled at the knees and fell over.

So I was the horse and Kenny was my rider and Fliss was on Lyndz's back and they were wobbling all over the place. Rosie told us to get ready because she was about to blow her whistle. And then we were off.

You have to dodge, like you do in

netball, which I'm ace at, and so I soon had Lyndz in the rose bushes. It's always the same really, a push-over. A barge-over, come to think of it. Good joke?

First we did the best of three, but the other team complained so much that we did the best of five. In the end, we did the best of fifteen and Kenny and I still won. Ea-sy! Just at the end I caught up with Lyndsey against the fence and barged her right up against it. Fliss and Kenny started wrestling, which is not really allowed but we'd already won, so it didn't seem to matter. It was lucky the fence was there because they both lost their balance and had to grab hold of it. But then they wouldn't let go. They were so interested In what was going on in next door's garden, we couldn't get them to move.

"Will you let go and come down?" Lyndz was yelling at Fliss.

"I'm dropping you if you don't," I threatened Kenny.

But they wouldn't take any notice of us, so we dumped them in the flower bed. They were both giggling so much neither of them could speak.

Then a man's very cross face appeared over the fence.

"Felicity, has your mother never taught you it's very rude to snoop and stare at people in the privacy of their own garden?"

Fliss just looked down and mumbled, "Sorry."

Kenny was nearly wetting herself.

"Well, I shall have to speak to her about this and the appalling noise you've been making. You're like a pack of wild animals."

And then the man's face disappeared and we all fled into the house like a... pack of wild animals, actually.

CHAPTER SIX

We couldn't wait to get back into Fliss's bedroom. We were dying to laugh. We rolled around the bed shrieking.

"Snoop and stare!"

"How could you snoop and stare?"

"Have you no manners?"

"What are you, wild animals?"

"He is seriously weird," said Kenny.

"But what was he doing?" I said.

"I don't know," said Kenny, "but whatever it was, he looked so stupid."

"He was standing there in his pyjamas," said Fliss, "doing these funny movements with his arms and legs."

"Like this," said Kenny, and she gave us a demonstration that looked like a robot.

Then we heard the front doorbell ring and we all hid our faces in our pillows and did a bit of silent screaming. The next thing we knew, Fliss's mum was coming upstairs. We quickly pulled ourselves together, all except Kenny. When Kenny starts, it's impossible for her to stop. And by now Lyndsey had got hiccups, as usual. So those two rushed out and escaped to the bathroom.

Fliss's mum was shaking her head and looking quite worried. We all felt guilty when we saw her face.

"Mr Watson-Wade's just been round to complain that you've been laughing at him while he was trying to do his Tai Chi."

"Tai Chi?" said Fliss. "What's that?"

"It's sort of exercises, movements; it's Chinese, I think. I don't know, but he says you have to be quiet and concentrate very hard while you're doing it and you girls completely disturbed him. It's supposed to be relaxing."

"Is that why he was wearing his pyjamas?" said Felicity.

"I've no idea, but I've apologised and I think tomorrow, Felicity, you had better go round and apologise yourself. I've told you about upsetting the neighbours."

Fliss just looked down and pulled a face. I didn't dare look at Rosie or I would have started off again. Rosie was sucking her thumb. I'd never seen her do that before but she said afterwards it was the only way she could stop herself from laughing.

"I think you'd better get ready for bed now."

"Aw, Mum, it's not very late," said Fliss.

"It's gone nine and I know you girls, by the time you're in bed it'll be gone ten. So I think you'd better start getting ready now."

Fliss's mum was right. It *was* gone ten

before we were in bed, because we do so much fooling around. At home I can get ready for bed in four minutes flat. I've timed it.

Starting from... now! Clothes off... and that's thirty seconds.

Pyjamas on and into the bathroom... and that's one minute gone.

Wet the flannel and a quick face and hands wipe... another thirty seconds. It takes a minute if you bother with the full soap treatment.

Then the slow bit: cleaning your teeth. Cap off the tube, quick squirt and brush, brush, brush, brush, brush, top and bottom. Gargle, gargle, quick spit out, dry your mouth... that's another minute gone.

Then leap on the loo... thirty seconds or a minute, depending on you know what.

Race back and leap into bed. Four minutes on the button!

When we're having a sleepover, things take a bit longer. Getting undressed, for a start. We always get undressed inside our sleeping bags. We *can* do it in two minutes, maybe a bit longer for me because I nearly fill the sleeping bag with my long arms and legs. But we usually take longer because we do this sort of invisible striptease. We wriggle down so we can't see each other and then we take off our clothes and throw them out at each other, especially our smelly socks. It's a great laugh.

We also spend a lot of time queueing to get into the bathroom and arguing about whose turn it is and waiting behind the bedroom door with a squishy-poo for whoever's last to come back.

Fliss was in her bed, Lyndz was in the spare bed, Rosie and Kenny and I were in a row in our sleeping bags on the floor between them. It was fine as long as the ones in the beds didn't try to get out of bed and step on our heads, and as long as the three of us didn't keep turning over and squashing each other.

Fliss's mum came in to say good night to us. "Have you girls got enough room there?"

"Yeah, we're fine," we told her.

"As snug as a bug," said Kenny.

"It's ever so late. I hope I'm not going to get into trouble with your mums," she said.

"Don't worry, Mrs Sidebotham. I never go to sleep at home before this time," I told her. "I'm a really late bird."

"You're a cuckoo," said Kenny. So I thumped her.

"Now settle down, girls," said Fliss's mum. She always has this worried look, so we did. She turned off the main light and closed the door. We lay very quiet and counted slowly to twenty until we were sure she'd gone and then we got our torches out.

"OK," said Rosie, "what are we going to do now?".

"Isn't it time to eat yet?" said Kenny.

"I'm ravenous."

"We've only just got into bed," said Fliss. "Let's have a game first. Or a story."

"But I'm starving," said Kenny.

"So am I," I said.

"Me too," said Rosie.

Lyndz said nothing, she just looked quiet, not a bit how she usually is. But the main thing was, Fliss was outvoted.

We all reached over and got out our food boxes. We passed them round and took a piece out of each. Well, Rosie and Kenny and I did. Fliss refused any pizza, she turned her nose up at the flapjack and she broke half a cheese straw off.

Lyndz was about to take her piece when she saw Fliss watching her. She just shook her head.

"Where's your popcorn?" I said.

Lyndz passed her box over.

"Great," said Kenny, until she saw it. "There's no sugar on this."

"Fewer calories," said Fliss.

Kenny passed it back without taking any.

Then Fliss passed a plastic bowl over. "Have some lemon surprise. It's out of the Weight Watchers cookbook. It's only twenty-five calories a portion."

"It tastes like lemon Jif," said Kenny, screwing up her face and almost spitting it out.

"Please yourself," said Fliss, eating some herself and then passing it to Lyndz.

Lyndz passed it back. "I'm not really hungry."

I was. Kenny and I had eaten our pieces of pizza *and* our flapjack *and* our cheese straws. In the end we even ate some of Lyndz's dry popcorn. We didn't eat any lemon Jif, thank you very much. We weren't that hungry.

I looked at the two pieces of pizza left in the box, but it seemed too greedy to eat those as well. I put the top back on the box, so it wouldn't be too tempting.

"What time is it?" asked Lyndsey.

"It's just gone eleven o'clock."

"What shall we do now?" I said.

"Tell us a story, Frankie," said Rosie.

"It'll have to be a short one," said Lyndsey. "I'm dead tired."

"A scary one," said Kenny.

"No, not a scary one," said Fliss. She hadn't got over the last time, when we'd scared ourselves silly talking to ghosts after Lyndz's birthday sleepover.

"I know," said Kenny. "Let's tell jokes. I'll go first, I've got a really good one. Why was the patient's cough better the next morning? Because he'd been practising all night."

"Shall I tell you the joke about the butter?" said Rosie. "I'd better not, you'll only spread it."

"Me next," I said. "Knock, knock."

"Who's there?"

"Howard."

"Howard who?"

"Howard you like to be outside for a change?"

Everybody groaned, but I'd got lots more like that.

"Knock, knock."
"Who's there?"
"Boo!"
"Boo-hoo?"
"Don't cry, it's only a joke."

CHAPTER SEVEN

I could have kept it up for hours but we heard Fliss's mum coming. We switched off our torches and lay with our eyes closed, pretending to be asleep. Kenny even did a bit of heavy breathing, which made us all start to giggle.

"Oh, dear, are you still awake?" she whispered. "You'll never be able to wake up tomorrow and I'll be in trouble with your mums. Now, please, settle down and go to sleep, there's good girls."

Then she went out and closed the door. But we still hadn't sung our going-to-sleep song, so we sat up in the torchlight and sang dead quietly, almost whispering:

"Down by the river there's a hanky-pankyyy,

With a bull-frog sitting near the hanky-pankyyy.

With an ooh-ahh, ooh-ahh, hey, Mrs Zippy, with a 1-2-3- OUT!"

We didn't sit up and do the actions. Everyone was too tired by now. Except me; I was still wide awake. I could hear Lyndz sucking her thumb and Fliss sniffing and Rosie wriggling about trying to get comfy. But I couldn't settle down.

I was feeling hungry. I know I'd had quite a lot to eat but I felt a bit like Winnie the Pooh. There was this little corner and I needed to fill it. I'd probably have been OK if I hadn't known there were two pieces of scrummy pizza just a few centimetres away. I could hear them calling my name.

You don't have to look at me like that. I'm not proud of it, but I just couldn't help myself. And they *were* mine, in a way. After all, I made them. Anyway, I ate them.

I heard midnight striking and then at last I fell asleep.

OK, let's sit down for a bit on this bench and I'll finish the story off before we get to Kenny's. Otherwise she'll start chipping in and spoiling it. And if any of the others are round at hers, they'll join in too.

When I woke up it was still dark, so for a minute I wasn't sure whether I'd been asleep at all. Lyndz had her hand on my shoulder and was whispering to me, "Frankie, are you awake?"

Then I realised I had been asleep but not for very long. It wasn't morning yet. It was starting to get light but it was very quiet so it must have been early. I turned over to face her and rubbed my eyes.

"I'm starving," she said. "Can I have my pizza now?"

I was glad Lyndz had come to her senses and wanted to eat again, but now I felt so guilty. I'd eaten both pieces of pizza and I felt a real pig.

"It's all gone," I whispered. "I'm sorry." And I really was.

"Gone where?" she whispered back.

But I didn't want to go into that, so I said. "Have some flapjack instead." I reached behind Kenny's head for her plastic box. It felt suspiciously light when I picked it up.

Yeah, you guessed right. That little porker had eaten the spare flapjack as well.

"Oh, no!" said Lyndz, when I showed her. "I'm so hungry."

By now I was wide awake and feeling I ought to do something about it, but I couldn't think what. I rolled over and shook Kenny and whispered in her ear, "Lyndz is starving, pass it on."

"What are you talking about, you mad woman?" said Kenny, as if it was part of her dream.

"It's your fault, you ate the flapjack, you little porker," I whispered. "Now pass it on."

So Kenny rolled over, shook Rosie, and whispered, "Lyndz is ravenous. Pass it on."

Rosie rubbed her eyes and whispered, "What time is it?"

"Never mind what time it is," hissed Kenny. "Just pass the cheese straws."

Rosie's face went bright pink. This can't be true, I thought, but it was.

"I ate them," she whispered.

"I don't believe it," said Kenny. She turned and whispered to me, "She ate them!"

"Well, tell her to pass it on," I whispered back.

So Rosie knelt up and shook Fliss. "Lyndz is dying of hunger."

Fliss groaned and turned over but Rosie kept shaking her until she sat up.

"Can't she eat the leftovers?" Fliss

hissed at us.

"There aren't any," I said. "And no, she doesn't want lemon Jif for breakfast."

By now we were all wide awake.

"What time is it?" said Fliss.

I turned on my torch and read my watch. "Half past four."

"Half past four! I can't wake my mum up at this time."

"Can't you go and get me something out of the fridge?" said Lyndz.

"Oh, honestly! I'm not your servant, you know." That is another thing about Fliss, she's very grumpy when she wakes up. "It's not my fault you're hungry."

"Well, it is, actually," I said.

"How d'you make that out?"

"If you hadn't got her started on this stupid diet stuff in the first place, she'd have had her pizza and flapjack and cheese straws while they were still there to eat. And she wouldn't be hungry now."

"So where are they? Who ate them?"

Rosie and Kenny and I put up our hands, as if we were at school.

"You are such pigs," said Fliss.

We all grunted in chorus.

"Well, aren't *you* hungry? You didn't have much either," Lyndz asked her.

Fliss went pink. "A bit."

"We're all hungry, actually," said Rosie.

"We need *food*," said Kenny.

Fliss got out of bed. "OK, but we'll have to be quiet. If we wake my mum and Andy, there'll be big trouble. Come on."

So we all tiptoed down the stairs and into the kitchen.

Rosie hadn't been in Fliss's kitchen yet, so she was really impressed with that as well. "This is amazing!" she said. "It's so new... and shiny... and modern! You should see mine. It's like something out of the Dark Ages. My mum would go wild if she saw this. You are so lucky."

Now there is nothing Fliss likes better than people telling her things like that.

"It's not new," she said. "We've had it for ages."

"Oh, and look! You've got a waffle-maker."

The truth is, Fliss's mum is mad on gadgets and every time we go there's something new. You name it, she's got it.

"Oh, can we have waffles?" Rosie begged. "Please. They're scrummy."

I thought Fliss would just go to the fridge and get us a yoghurt or make a sandwich or something. Not on your life. Fliss was determined to impress everyone, Rosie especially. She put on her mum's apron and said, "Right, what do the rest of you want?" Just as if she was taking orders in McDonald's.

"Porridge."

"Toast."

"Milkshake."

"OK," she said.

"Can you really do all that?" said Lyndz.

"Seriously?" said Rosie. "Are you allowed?"

"Yeah," said Fliss. "My mum lets me do anything in the kitchen."

"Even waffles?" I said, suspiciously.

"We-ell, the waffle-maker's new. I'm not so sure about that."

"I can do waffles," said Kenny. "My auntie's got one."

"I can do the toast," said Lyndz. "Where's the bread?"

"I'll do the milkshakes," said Rosie.

Soon they were all racing round the kitchen, opening cupboards, in and out of the fridge. I sat on one of the high bar stools, watching. To tell you the truth, I was feeling a bit icky. Not exactly sick, you know, just a bit, urghhh. But old Bossy-boots spotted me.

"Don't just sit there, Frankie," she said. "You set the table."

"OK." I slid down and started to search for table mats and cutlery and ketchup and anything else I could think of. If we were going to have a party, we might as well have a proper one.

For my Brownie Hostess badge I'd had to lay a table and make a table decoration. I found some candlesticks and I looked round for something else I could use. I thought I'd better not ask Fliss; everyone else was already firing questions at her.

"Where's the salt?"

"Can I use these bananas?"

"Is this the only milk you've got?"

"Haven't you got any sliced bread?"

"I don't know," she snapped back. "You'll have to look. I can't do everything." She was getting in a razz because she'd spilled porridge oats all over the table. I tried to help her but she said, "I can manage. I've done this lots of times, you know."

So I tried to help Rosie with the milkshakes. She let me slice a banana, big deal! But then she said *she* wanted to do the mixing. So I watched Lyndz have three attempts at cutting a slice of bread. Every time she ended up with a wedge that looked like a dry ski slope and a pile of breadcrumbs you could have stuffed a mattress with.

"Oh, go away, Frankie! It's because you're watching me. You're putting me off."

So I watched Kenny instead, whisking this mixture of eggs and milk so fast most of it shot up in the air and all over the worktop.

"Look out!" I said.

"Look out yourself," she said. "Give me some room, can't you?"

"Keep your voices down," Fliss whispered above the noise. "You'll wake everyone."

Just then we heard footsteps on the stairs. We all stopped what we were doing and tried to hide things behind our backs. We stood still and froze to the spot, watching the kitchen door handle turn, expecting to see Fliss's mum's face or, even worse, Andy's. We were madly trying to think of a good excuse.

But when the door opened, it was Callum, Fliss's little brother, otherwise known as the Pest, standing in the doorway. He was rubbing his eyes and yawning. "What're you lot doing?" he said.

We all let out a sigh and relaxed. The worst danger was over. Now we just had to deal with him.

CHAPTER EIGHT

Fliss rushed over and dragged Callum into the kitchen and closed the door behind him. "Shhh! Keep your voice down," she hissed at him. "You're not supposed to be up at this time."

"Neither are you."

"You'll get into trouble if Mum and Andy wake up."

"So will you."

"What do you want, anyway?"

His eyes travelled round the kitchen. "I'm hungry."

"Join the club," said Lyndsey.

"All right, sit down and don't move," said Fliss. "We'll make you some breakfast if you swear you'll keep quiet and behave."

"You know I'm not allowed to swear."

"Oh, very funny," said Fliss, in a tired voice. "Just sit there and stay out of our way." Then she went back to the porridge preparations.

I sat opposite Callum and watched him. I've often wanted a sister but I've never really wanted a brother, especially a younger brother like Callum.

"What're you staring at?" he said.

"I don't know," I said, "the label's fallen off."

"Get me a drink," he said and, like an idiot, I did.

After that, since everyone else was busy slicing and chopping and stirring and slopping things in all directions and wouldn't let me join in, I thought I'd go out into the garden to pick a few flowers to make the table look nice.

Quick, the toaster's on fire!

I went to the back door but there was no key in the lock. I looked everywhere I could think it might be: on a hook, like at my house, on a shelf, in a drawer in the hall stand. But it wasn't there. So I went back into the kitchen to ask Fliss.

In those few moments I'd been gone, the kitchen had turned into a disaster area. The thick chunk of toast that Lyndz had cut was now stuck in the toaster and smoke was coming out of it. Luckily we'd all done our Home Safety badge.

"Turn it off!" squealed Fliss.

"At the plug!" we all squealed together.

"I know, I know," she squealed back.

But the smoke had set off the smoke alarm and now it was flashing and pinging.

"Someone wave a newspaper at it," said Fliss. "Quick, before it wakes my mum."

Fliss was busy watching her porridge frothing in the microwave, so I grabbed a magazine and waved it in the air until the alarm went silent.

For a couple of seconds everything was quiet. I was just about to ask Fliss where the back-door key was kept when Kenny let out a cry. I'd watched her pouring the mixture into the waffle-maker and I'd thought it looked sort of thin. Now it was running down the sides and all over the work surface and down the cupboard doors. A little pool on the floor at her feet was already turning into a river.

"Look what you're doing!" squealed Fliss. "Get a cloth and clear it up."

"Where will I find one?" said Kenny.

"I'll get it," I said, rushing to the sink at exactly the same moment Fliss bent to get one out of the cupboard. We banged heads.

"Oh, thanks very much," she shouted at me.

"It was an accident," I shouted back.

But there was no time to worry about the small matter of two cracked skulls because by now Fliss's porridge was bubbling over the side of the bowl and frothing all over the microwave. It reminded me of that bit in *Gremlins* when one of the gremlins gets put in the microwave. Gruesome.

"Oh no! Now look what you've made me do!" Fliss screamed at Kenny.

"*I* made you do?" Kenny screamed back.

This could have turned into a **big** one, but just then another disaster struck.

Rosie had been having a great time chopping loads of fruit: apples and raisins and a few nuts she'd found in the cupboard. In fact, anything she could lay her hands on. She'd poured a whole bottle of milk into the liquidiser and was ready to turn it on. She was sniffing the mixture, which looked and smelt delicious. And it would have been, I'm sure, if she'd had the sense to put the lid on properly.

Unfortunately, she didn't. Right in the middle of Fliss and Kenny's argument, the liquidiser lid flew up in the air and hit the fridge door. Milkshake hit the room at fifty miles an hour, most of it landing on Rosie. It coated her hair and face so that she looked like something out of *Gremlins* too.

"Oh, my God, what have you done?" Fliss shrieked at Rosie.

"Boy, are you gonna be in trouble when my mum sees this," said Callum. The little toad was grinning from ear to ear.

"Shut up!" Fliss hissed at him. "Just get it all cleaned up now," she yelled at the rest of us.

I'd already tried to help Kenny clean up the waffle mess but she'd just pushed me out of the way. And now Fliss was giving Rosie a big lecture, so I thought, OK, I'm out of here. They can all do their own cleaning-up. I hadn't made any of the mess. It wasn't my fault.

So I went out into the hall and suddenly had this brainwave. I thought, I can get into the garden through the patio doors in the lounge. So I did. And that was the reason I wasn't around when Kenny had her accident – can you believe it, I *still* managed to get the blame for it.

I heard all about it afterwards, a dozen times at least, so I can tell you exactly what happened. And I suppose Fliss was right, it wouldn't have happened if I'd stayed in the kitchen.

All the time the liquidiser was throwing milkshake over Rosie's head, and the porridge was erupting in the microwave, and the waffle mixture was running down the cupboards, Lyndz was trying to toast a second slab of toast and, surprise, surprise, that got stuck as well. This time the toaster smoked even worse and a couple of flames came out of it.

"Turn it off!" Fliss squealed again.

"At the plug!" Rosie and Kenny joined in.

But this time it had caused so much smoke that even though they all waved newspapers and magazines in the air, the smoke alarm wouldn't stop. That's why I got the blame. None of them was tall enough to reach the alarm, so it went on pinging and flashing.

"Now you're going to be for it," said Callum again.

Well, Fliss nearly went haywire. "Shut up!" she shouted at him. "Just shut up! Oh, please, can't somebody make that stop?" she begged the others.

So Kenny jumped up on one of the bar stools, taking swipes at it with a magazine.

"Die, you alien!" she said, swiping furiously.

"Oh, stop fooling around, Kenny," said Lyndz.

"She's going to fall in a minute," said Rosie.

"Oh, where's Frankie, for goodness' sake?" yelled Fliss.

CHAPTER NINE

Good question! Well, in fact, at exactly that same moment, after a lot of fiddling, I had just managed to unlock the patio door. This turned out to be a *big* mistake and was the second reason I got the blame for everything, even though I wasn't there.

This dreadful noise started up and I nearly died. No, it wasn't the smoke alarm. That was gentle and quite soothing compared with this din. This was the burglar alarm. I'd set it off opening the patio doors.

I didn't know what to do. I tried closing the door again but it didn't make any difference. It still went on blaring away.

I mean, what would you have done? I didn't know whether to close the door, sneak back in the kitchen and pretend it had nothing to do with me, or rush out into the garden and find somewhere to hide. So I was stuck there, half in and half out, like a burglar in the middle of a smash-and-grab raid that's gone wrong.

Back in the kitchen things were even worse. Perhaps it was the shock of hearing the burglar alarm that panicked Kenny. Whatever it was, she took one big swipe at the smoke alarm and fell off the stool. Lyndz tried to catch her, missed, and they both landed on the floor in a heap with Kenny's arm underneath them.

And then everyone went to pieces. They could hear the burglar alarm blaring away and now they could hear the sound of Fliss's mum and Andy getting out of bed.

"Uh-oh," said Callum, looking like the cat that's got the cream. "Trouble."

Standing there with the porridge bowl in her hands, Fliss took one look around the kitchen. There was a smell of burning again, but this time it wasn't the toaster, it was coming from the waffle-maker. When Rosie opened it, out popped four rubber waffles.

There were already two fat rounds of black toast on the worktop that were so burnt you could have played football with them.

"What am I going to do?" Fliss whimpered. "They'll go mad."

Lyndz was trying to help Kenny up. By now she'd realised it wasn't just a bit of a bump they'd had and she could see Kenny's arm was really hurting. Fliss was in shock and Callum was no use whatsoever. So that only left Rosie. Luckily she took charge.

She grabbed the rubber waffles and the burnt toast and dumped them in the porridge bowl and charged out of the kitchen with them. She rushed into the hall just as I was coming back in.

"Where are you going?" I asked her.

"Quick," she said. "We've got to get rid of the evidence."

"Into the garden," I said. "This way." And I led her out through the patio doors. The noise was even worse outside.

"What's going on?" I shouted.

"Someone set off the alarm," she shouted back at me.

Even then I could see how funny we must look, both standing there in our pyjamas, shouting at each other and holding all this burnt food. Suddenly we saw Fliss's mum and Andy through the kitchen window so we ducked round the corner out of sight.

"What are we going to do with this?" said Rosie, holding the bowl out in front of her.

Now, I know the sensible thing would have been to dump it all in the dustbin, but the dustbin was round the other side of the house and we didn't dare go past the windows in case they saw us. And anyway, at half past five in the morning I wasn't feeling very sensible.

"Oh, Frankie, what are we going to do with it?" Rosie said again.

Why is it that people always expect me to come up with ideas?

Yeah, yeah, I know. Because I always do.

We were standing close to the next door's fence, so, without thinking much about it, I flung the two burnt slabs of toast over the fence into the Grumpies' garden and then threw the waffles after them.

"What are you doing?" Rosie shrieked. I just grinned. I thought it was a neat idea.

Now we were just left with the bowl of porridge. This wasn't ordinary porridge that you can pour out of a pan, this was Fliss's specially constructed quick-set cement porridge. You'd have needed a knife and fork to eat it. So I just turned the bowl upside down and it fell on the grass in a solid ball.

For a second Rosie stood looking at it. Then she started grinning too. She picked it up and hurled it over the fence after the toast and waffles.

We suddenly realised that it had all gone quiet. The alarm had been turned off.

I was still holding the bowl when Fliss's mum came through the patio doors.

"Come in, this minute!" she called. "You'll catch your death of cold."

And that was the first time we noticed that it really was freezing.

When we got in, we soon realised we'd only got rid of some of the evidence. There was plenty more of it left in the kitchen. But nobody seemed to bother much about the mess, they were far more worried about Kenny's accident.

Poor old Kenny was a funny grey colour by the time we got in. Andy strapped up her arm before he took her to the hospital. I couldn't work out for the life of me how you could get a broken arm just making waffles. Rosie gave me the full story while we were sitting in Casualty waiting for Kenny to have her arm set.

Fliss and her mum and Lyndz stayed at home to look after Callum and do the clearing-up. Andy took me and Rosie with him to Leicester Infirmary, because it was still only six o'clock and too early to deliver us home on a Sunday morning.

I couldn't believe so much had happened in only an hour. We all sat as quiet as mice in the car. When the nurse called Kenny's name, Andy went in with her to get her arm X-rayed, because her mum and dad hadn't arrived yet. So then Rosie had the chance to tell me the bits I'd missed while I was busy breaking out of Fliss's house.

"But what were you doing to set the alarm off in the first place?" said Rosie.

"I was trying to pick some flowers," I said. And I knew as soon as I said it that it sounded a pathetic excuse.

It was half past eight before we got back from the hospital. Kenny's mum and dad had come to take her home. She was fine. She'd loved every minute of it. Kenny adores hospitals. She's weird that way. She's hurt her arm a couple of times before but never badly enough to have a plaster, so she was mega-excited and couldn't wait to go to school to get everyone to sign it.

We were just relieved it was all over. Because everyone had been so worried about Kenny, we'd not really been told off much... until we got back to Fliss's! When we saw her mum's face, we could tell there was plenty to come. Boy, was she in a razz!

GOODBYE

Andy had been quite good fun on the way back in the car. He was starting to tease us about trying to get us on these new TV programmes: *Ready Steady, Wreck the Kitchen* and *Can't Cook, Better Not Cook Ever Again* and silly things like that. So we all went into the house smiling.

Fliss tried to warn us. She waved her hands nervously at us from behind her mum, who stood in the kitchen doorway with her arms folded and a cross expression on her face. They must have worked hard because the kitchen was back to normal. It was all smart and shiny and gleaming cream behind her.

Then she moved and beckoned us to follow. The only thing that was out of place and completely spoiled the effect was a tray sitting in the middle of the worktop with two large slabs of burnt toast on it and four rubber waffles and a football made out of porridge. The only difference between now and the last time we'd seen them was that then they were dry and now they were soaking wet.

"Mr Watson-Wade has just been round," she said, talking between her teeth. "And brought these with him. It seems he fished them out of his pond. I don't suppose either of you two happens to know how they got there?"

Sometimes honesty is *definitely* the best policy. We just came clean and owned up. We got a serious earwigging from Fliss's mum. Kenny got off lightest, because of her arm. Fliss got into most trouble because it seems she is definitely not allowed, no way, under no circumstances, to do any cooking whatsoever without her mum there to supervise. Well, that was news to us! She was banned from cooking *for ever*. Or at least until her mum forgets about it, which won't be soon.

Of course, when the rest of our parents heard the story, they all said the same thing, more or less, so that puts all of us out of the Brownie competition.

But the good news is Lyndz has stopped talking about stupid diets. She was sick of it anyway and now she's back to her old self, with her smily face and her happy knees, and we're all glad about that.

Fliss has learnt her lesson too. She never talks about diets any more either, we've cured her of that. Whenever she mentions it, we all start yawning and tell her she's really bor-ing. Now we have great midnight feasts again and sleepovers are back to normal. Thank goodness!

At first Fliss and I had a mega-row when she tried to make out it had all been my fault. She said that if I hadn't made her feel guilty, she'd never have taken us down to the kitchen. And if I hadn't gone out of the kitchen, I'd have been there to stop the smoke alarm, and if I'd been in the kitchen with the rest of them, I couldn't have been in the lounge setting off the burglar alarms and waking up her mum and Andy and getting us all caught.

That's her side of the story. This is mine: if she hadn't started Lyndz on this stupid diet, we'd all have had plenty to eat, Lyndz wouldn't have woken up in the middle of the night starving, we wouldn't have gone down into the kitchen, Fliss wouldn't have started showing off and pretending she could cook things she couldn't, we wouldn't have had any disasters and Rosie and I wouldn't have needed to dispose of the evidence. So there, now you've heard both sides and you can decide.

Oh, look! Lyndz's bike is outside Kenny's house so that means she's there. You'll be able to meet her at last. And Kenny might let you sign her plaster. Just your name, mind, no rude jokes; she's already got into trouble for that. She let Ryan Scott write on it at school. I did warn her. But that's Kenny for you. Completely barmy.

Come on, let's go in. I can't wait for you to meet them.

The Sleepover Club at Frankie's

Join the Sleepover Club: Frankie, Kenny, Felicity, Rosie and Lyndsey, five girls who just want to have fun – but who always end up in mischief.

Brown Owl's in a bad mood and the Sleepover Club are determined to cheer her up. Maybe she'd be happier if she had a new boyfriend. And where better than a sleepover at Frankie's to plan Operation Blind Date?

Pack up your sleepover kit and drop in on the fun!

0 00 675233 0

The Sleepover Club
at Lyndsey's

Join the Sleepover Club: Frankie, Kenny, Felicity, Rosie and Lyndsey, five girls who just want to have fun – but who always end up in mischief.

The girls plan a great party for Lyndsey's birthday – fun, food, a spooky video and a sleepover. Definitely not for boys! But somehow Lyndsey's brothers make their presence felt and soon everyone's too scared to sleep.

Pack up your sleepover kit and drop in on the fun!

0 00 675234 9

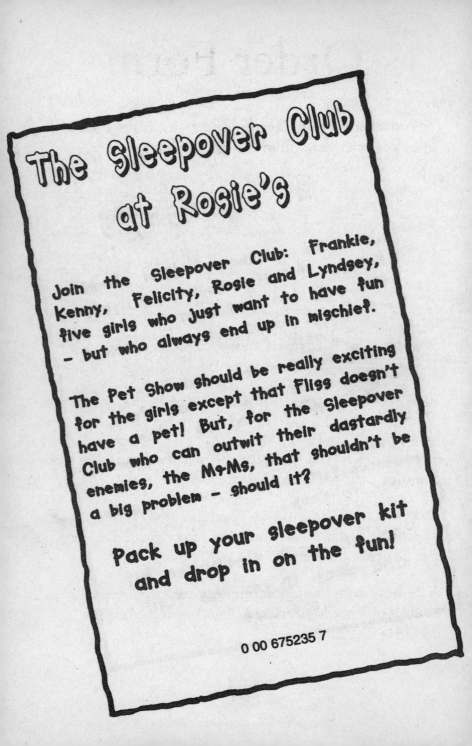

The Sleepover Club at Rosie's

Join the Sleepover Club: Frankie, Kenny, Felicity, Rosie and Lyndsey, five girls who just want to have fun – but who always end up in mischief.

The Pet Show should be really exciting for the girls except that Fliss doesn't have a pet! But, for the Sleepover Club who can outwit their dastardly enemies, the M&Ms, that shouldn't be a big problem – should it?

Pack up your sleepover kit and drop in on the fun!

0 00 675235 7

Order Form

To order direct from the publishers, just make a list of the titles you want and fill in the form below:

Name ....

Address ....

....

....

Send to: Dept 6, HarperCollins Publishers Ltd, Westerhill Road, Bishopbriggs, Glasgow G64 2QT.

Please enclose a cheque or postal order to the value of the cover price, plus:

UK & BFPO: Add £1.00 for the first book, and 25p per copy for each additional book ordered.

Overseas and Eire: Add £2.95 service charge. Books will be sent by surface mail but quotes for airmail despatch will be given on request.

A 24-hour telephone ordering service is available to holders of Visa, MasterCard, Amex or Switch cards on 0141- 772 2281.

HarperCollins *Children's Books*